The Impatient Caterpillar

Cynthia Hickey

ISBN:978-1-959788-55-3

Dedicated to Alyssah! Go and enrich minds.

Meet Alyssah.

Alyssah was a butterfly.

Well, maybe not exactly a butterfly. She was actually just a chubby little caterpillar.

Her mommy told her that someday she would be a beautiful butterfly, but Alyssah didn't believe her.

When she looked in the mirror, all she saw was a caterpillar.

Every morning when she woke up, the first thing she would do was look in the mirror to see if anything had changed.

Her mommy told her it would happen while she was sleeping. But when? Alyssah had waited a very long time already.

On school days, Alyssah would grab her backpack and her mommy would say,

"God makes everything beautiful in its time. Your time will come. You're perfect just as you are."

Alyssah wasn't completely convinced, but she didn't have time to argue. Today was a very special day.

It was the first day of a brand new school year!
SCHOOL

All her friends were there!
Lucy the ladybug with her
polka-dotted coat.

Alyssah wanted to go fast like Betty the bumblebee.

She really liked David the dragonfly's shiny clothes.

But she was just a chubby, pink, little caterpillar.

Most days, all her friends got to school much faster than she did. Sometimes it was already recess by the time she arrived.
SCHOOL

This made Alyssah go off by herself.

Sometimes, her big brother would give her a ride home! This made her feel like she could fly!

But he would tell her the same thing their mother did. "Be patient. You'll be a butterfly in time." Alyssah wanted to be one now!

Then one morning, it happened!

She looked in
the mirror and
saw...

A butterfly with pretty pink wings. Her mother and brother were right!

All she had to do was be patient. Alyssah was beautiful!

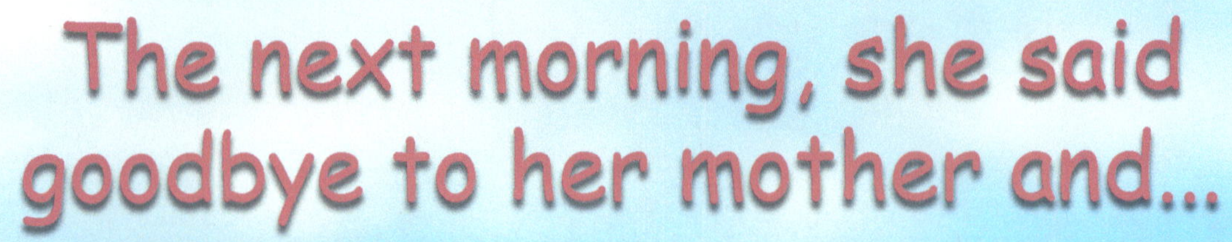

The next morning, she said
goodbye to her mother and...

Tried out her new wings!

Now she beat all her friends to school.

When they all arrived, they cheered for her!

Now Alyssah wants you to know
that you are perfect and beautiful.
Just as God created you.

Alyssah was a cute, chubby caterpillar. But, she wanted to be a butterfly, and she didn't want to wait! Everyone told her to be patient, that she'd be a butterfly when it was time.

Join along as Alyssah and her friends learn that good things come to those who wait.

ISBN 978-1-959788-55-3
9 781959 788553

The Legend of the
Goose Girl

By Rupert Procter

Illustrations by
Nathalie Madron